# Amico di Sandro

Frederick William Rolfe, a.k.a. Baron Corvo (1860–1913), was born in Cheapside, London. In 1886, he converted to Roman Catholicism. His short stories were published in various periodicals, including the *Yellow Book*. He wrote *A History of the Borgias* (1901), as well as a number of novels, the most famous of them being *Hadrian the Seventh* (1904). He died in poverty in Venice.

# FREDERICK ROLFE

⚜

## BARON CORVO

# AMICO DI SANDRO

THIS IS A SNUGGLY BOOK

This edition Copyright © 2019
by Snuggly Books.

All rights reserved.

ISBN: 978-1-64525-000-5

# AMICO DI SANDRO

'OH, I do think that I ought to know something about Friendship. I had a friend, once. But he died.'

'If it would not grieve you to speak of him . . .' I began.

'No. You see, he died exactly four hundred and one years ago.'

I sat up (I fear) a little cataclysmically.

'You are not by any chance a silly fool—are you?' he asked, sticking in his monocle, and gravely regarding me.

'Oh I hope not. But—can you remember?' I asked. 'Can I forget, you mean. No. Never. Are you sure that it won't bore you, though?'

'I should like to hear it immensely,' I said.

'M—yes:' he agreed, ending his scrutiny. 'I really believe that you would. I even fancy that you may understand.'

He dropped his eyeglass; and yawned; and looked across the blue lagoon; and began to speak, astoundingly, but deliberately, and as one who reads something written on the sky.

Sandro gushed out of a shop in front of me, just as I put the bread-basket down. My idea had been to rest a bit, before I faced the gusts of wintry wind which blow through the arches of Ponte Vecchio. I was broken-hearted that morning. A little chap of ten doesn't have much of a time, when he is the slave of a brutal baker like Toccio. Everyone else seemed to have parents of some sort. But I had no one. Why, I hadn't even a name, till I chose one, later. And, when Sandro burst out of the house in front of me, I couldn't help wondering what he did in the street at that early hour. Other people's affairs interested me: because I had none of my own. I suppose I looked at him rather fixedly. He was such a big strong boy, to me—five years my senior, he told me, when we compared histories. And he had been in a towering rage, when he leaped out of the shop and all but stumbled over me. I always did stare at everything; and I was always getting thrashed for it by someone or another. About the first thing I can remember is an awful thrashing which I took from Toccio when Luca Pitti was Gonfalonier. Geronimo di Agnolo Machiavelli had been coughing at Luca's violent tyranny. Arrested and exiled, he tried to get help from the neighbouring nations. But Luca was bold and rich and powerful enough to capture him before he did any mischief, and at the Palazzo del Podesta they tormented him so forcibly that he made an end of living out of pure displeasure and melancholy. The aspect of his corpse, when Luca Pitti was satisfied with it, became talked about in Toccio's shop. Everybody wondered why Cosimo Medici let such things happen. They said that he preferred to live quietly in Via Larga with the society of learned men and to build churches peaceably. They said, also, that he ought to beware, because Luca was enlisting malefactors and bandits to garrison those two huge new palaces which he made one inside the walls and another a mile beyond. And then Toccio turned, caught me staring, and battered me properly over his knees with the mixing bat. I must have been about eight years old then. And, when they buried our Archbishop I got another thrashing. Everybody loved Saint Antonino. What an adorable face he had! I can

see it now. They said that he left nothing behind him, not even a silver spoon: he had given
everything to the poor. Even Toccio blubbered
when that blessed body went by to burial; and
then turned and thrashed me for staring. But
I didn't care—I had learned what lines make
the face of a Saint. And of course, when the
Pontiff came, two days after the Festival of
Saint George, my thrashings became diurnal.
Various sovereigns carried the throne of His
Holiness with pomp unspeakable through the
city to Santa Maria Novella where He lodged;
and I took a thrashing for staring at His
progress. We had a hunt in Piazza Santacroce
for His amusement—wolves, lions, boars, and
one giraffe. Naturally I forgot my breadbasket
and took a thrashing for remembrance. Then
there was the burial of the Cardinal of Lisbon
who died in our city on a journey for Pope
Pio. They buried him outside, at San Miniato,
very ceremoniously because he was royal and
a cousin of the Empress Leonora. Toccio
thrashed me when I came back from Por San
Miniato whither I had followed the pageant;
and then began to gossip with the neighbours
concerning the dead. He need not have died,
they said, if he would have consented to couple,

as his doctors desired: but he preferred a clean death to a contaminated life. I, at ten, thought this saying very strange; and instantly Toccio battered me strongly for staring. You may imagine that I was fairly fed up with thrashings in my second year as a baker's boy; and it so happened that I was seriously thinking of making a change of some kind. I had had enough; and I wanted something new. The fact is that I had a sort of plan in my head. First, you must understand that, what with staring and what with listening, I was full to bursting with all sorts of ideas and all sorts of images; and I was in a fever to make something of them. Do you know that many of my thrashings were for shaping faces out of dough—faces like the faces of people whom I had seen, and the same faces as I would have liked them to be? How Toccio did rage about an image which I made of him, with his wen beneath his eye and his series of undulating chins! Second, you should know that people were talking much just then about the new abbey which Cosimo Medici was building outside Por San Gallo at Fiesole. He was building the church of San Geronimo there too, to say nothing of a church for the friars minor at Mugello, and the church of San

Lorenzo and the church of San Frediano and the convent and church of San Marco all in the city. But, for some reason or other, I only thought of the abbey at Fiesole. And I also heard much talk of him, not only as being as rich if not richer than Luca Pitti, but also as being a very much more gentle man, taking his pleasure in collecting youths who could do things with their hands, or their minds, and letting them do them. My idea, then, was to wait till Toccio had made me bleed again; and then to run away for refuge to the abbey of Fiesole, where someone surely would pity me. And the Pontiff was going to pass through Fiorenza, on this bitter morning at the end of January, as he returned to Rome; and I determined to deliver the contents of my bread-basket early, and then to follow the procession through the city, obtaining as many apostolic benedictions as possible, for my comfort when Toccio should batter me forcibly on my return to Via Ghibellina: after which I was to crawl as best I could to Fiesole. I made this plan while I was gently feeling the blue weals on my thighs the whole night long, soothing their burning with the coolness of my hand.

I stared at Sandro; and Sandro stared at me. He wasn't quite a stranger. Going about the city as I did, I had seen him many times before, and no one could help noticing him. You see, he was always alone, never crowded with companions like other boys. I thought him proud, for that, and for his bold disdainful carriage. He was so tall that his head seemed to condescend to me. And nothing could possibly be grander than the splendour of his blazing hair and the whiteness of his skin and the sad fierce masterfulness of his big brown eyes. I was frightfully afraid of him: but I stared and stared. As I said, at first he burst upon me in a towering rage. As we looked at each other, eyes joined to eyes, rays to rays; and strong ligations were effected. His fierceness vanished. His sadness remained. O that fine octagonal face of his—the great dark thoughtful eyes the straight broad nose pointed at its low tip—the wide firm mouth with its full lower lip, curbed by the very thin bow of the upper—the very square strong jaw—the expression insolent because modest, imperious because shy,—but a face which could smile. And O the robust and generous young form, noble and opulent in contour—the ardent force restrained of him. To me, from the beginning, he was something apart, an individual whom one must either abhor, or adore—nothing else—and, as I saw him close for the first time, staring at him quite unreservedly, I knew what my feelings were. The ideas of Cosimo and the abbey of Fiesole went— piph—paph. I believe that I never thought of them again till this moment. Sandro suddenly asked me why I stared at him. And all unpremeditatedly I burst out crying and flung myself at him hugging his leg, saying the only words which came to me, that I admired the thick swathes of his red hair. At first he thought that I was mocking him: for it seemed that everyone else in the world derided him for the very thing which I deemed so supremely beautiful. Judas Ischarioth, they said, had red hair, which of course is a lie: for Messer Domeniddio is too exquisite an artist to give beautiful features to persons with ugly minds. Sandro shook me, till, what with the wounds of the day before and the emotions of that wintry morning, I believe that I swooned away. Anyhow, I let him shake me: but I never let go of his leg; and the next thing I remember is lying in his lap, with his arms embracing me, his lips on mine, and a torrent of such gentle words as I had never heard before pouring into my ears. And that was my meeting with Sandro.

As we sat on the doorstep, I think we told each other everything. It appeared that we were both sick of our mode of lives, and were resolved to change them. So far we were alike. The difference between us was that I had no parents and that he had plenty. But he declared that his were no use to him. He flatly refused to work in the tan-yard of Ser Mariano his father: and he detested working in the precious metals for his brother Giovanni, to whom he had been apprenticed these three years. He was tired, he said, of sitting bent double all day, chiselling and punching and pinching little tiny gold things. What he wanted was to do something larger. Not that his parents were unkind. Oh no. But Ser Mariano was always grieving because he was so eccentric. And Giovanni had lately married Mona Nera di Benineasa di Manno di Cori; and very likely would soon be having a family of his own to keep. As Sandro told me this, someone came quickly on the bridge toward us. It was Giovanni; and he began to curse Sandro wildly for staying out all night and consorting with the scum of the city. I was for grabbing my bread-basket and scooting: but Sandro seized my hand and held me while he answered his brother. He said that he hadn't been out all night. On the contrary he had stayed so late in the shop working on the necklace for Mona Landomia di Iacopo Acciajuoli, that he fell asleep there as soon as he had finished it. And as for consorting with the scum of the city, he had never done such a thing in his life nor would begin now. On the contrary, the youth present was his friend, and quite willing to come and work in the shop in place of Giobbe who went to Pisa last week after a girl. Sandro spoke with his head a little on one side and his big eyes looking coolly at Giovanni, and his lips drawn thin with resolution. His tone was keen—not menacing, but there were menaces behind it. Giovanni, of whom I have nothing to complain, looked me over: at the mention of the finished necklace he had given a little start; and when Sandro ceased from speaking he said nothing but went into his shop. We followed. The lamp was still burning and the place thick with oily fumes. Giovanni opened the windows to let in the morning air; and extinguished the lamp as he looked at the necklace lying in a litter of tools on the banco. He was five years older than Sandro, a small lean young man with no likeness to his brother excepting in his grave demeanour. But, whereas Sandro's gravity was due to his spirit of masterful and generally disdainful inquisitiveness which concentrated the plenitude of his tremendous forces on that which at the moment interested him, Giovanni had the simple seriousness of the ordinary respectable and very useful ass. Sandro's was the intellectual gravity of an examining magistrate: Giovanni's, that of the ordinary expert tormentor. Sandro was an investigator of causes: Giovanni dealt mechanically with effects. He took up the necklace and inspected it. It was of the pattern of most of the necklaces which came out of his shop, a design of Sandro's of course, just a number of little bottles made of gems and gold linked together by light chains. Giovanni got his nickname of Botticello from these little bottles. When things were settled I made many of them myself. It was not difficult. Anybody can make gold chains. But Giovanni Botticello's necklaces depended, for their beauty and value, on the care with which he matched the roundish-oval pearls which formed the body of the little bottles. A woman would come and order a necklace of five or ten or twenty bottles, according to the state of her husband's or her lover's pouch. We then matched the necessary pearls, fitted them with base and bands and bottle-neck of gold, set a ruby in the top of each neck to simulate wine, linked the necks on light chains so that the pearl belly of the bottle dangled down, and there she had her necklace. Mona Landomia's was a splendid one of thirty little bottles, but then she was an Acciajuoli and married to Cosimo Medici's own nephew Pierfrancesco. While Giovanni peered at the work Sandro coolly went on talking. He simply said that he wouldn't stay another moment in Giovanni's employment unless I were given the runaway Giobbe's situation and a place in the family house in Por Santamaria. As for being liable to the torments provided for unruly apprentices Sandro mentioned that he was only working for Giovanni to please his father and without indentures; and that he was determined to run away to the Pisan War within three minutes if the present simple little matter were not arranged to his satisfaction on the instant. Giovanni said that Sandro was a problem; and, mounting his stool, began his morning's work. At which, Sandro took me and the bread-basket back to Via Ghibellina, he bidding Toccio to find another slave or to deliver his nutriment himself, I being no longer available; and I spent the morning tidying-up the Botticello shop on Ponte Vecchio, whilst Sandro and Giovanni went on making their precious little bottles. At midday we shut the shop and went to the house in Por Santamaria to eat. Beside Giovanni and Mona Nera, there was Ser Mariano Filipepi the tanner, a jolly citizen of thirty-seven years old who couldn't possibly be unkind of anybody, and his other son Antonio, a year younger than Sandro, and a wise youth with a mania for fingering the books of learned persons. It seemed that Sandro did pretty much as he liked in the house of the family; and, when he said that I was his friend and fellow-worker, everybody smiled at me, specially Mona Nera. She, though, was for boiling water instantly; and would have washed me then and there; but Sandro did it behind a screen in the kitchen—at least he got my rags off, and me in the tub, and then yelled so hideously at the sight of my back and thighs, that everyone ran to aid. I never saw anything so devastating as his fury. He gnashed his teeth, roaring selected maledictions, stamping his feet, waving his arms and whirling like a quintain.

Ser Mariano cursed slightly at first; and then turned round, and sent Antonio flying upstairs to find an unguent which he said was sovereign. And Giovanni said that Antonio might as well bring also some of his own old clothes to serve till I could be properly fitted. But Mona Nera took off her sleeves, and went down on her dear knees to me and washed me all over in the tub. I never had a mother and I had never before been touched by a woman; and I'm afraid that I rather resented being treated like a baby. Only for a minute though: for she was so gently irresistible, and her sweet eyes looked so tenderly, and the delicious odour of her was so strange and so intoxicating as she handled me that I burst out crying again. Ser Mariano chuckled and said that I would do finely for a baby for Mona Nera till she got one of her own, at which she blushed and looked at Giovanni. And then Sandro mastered himself and took me in hand. Did I say that I was a dark-skinned black-haired rosy child? I always remember colours. The clothes which Antonio brought me were white and brown—thick white knitted hose, brown leather shoes, brown leather jerkin, with two thick white woollen shirts and of course a Vermilion cap. Everybody wore vermilion caps then: but I couldn't put mine on, because Sandro tied my hair up to dry in a towel while we sat at table. How those good people fed me! Soup with vast gobbets of real meat in it, as much white bread as I could devour and a big beaker of red wine. What with one thing and what with another, I was on the verge of blubbering again. Things seemed hard to swallow, somehow. But Sandro solemnly said that if I howled Mona Nera would kiss me. So I just choked and fell upon my portion. Ser Mariano said I was a man. Rot, isn't it? No? Ah I thought you weren't a fool.

People began to run, shouting, along the street. It was the Pontiff passing. Poor old Pontiff! How cold He looked! The white mule which He had ridden up to the city-gate was led in front of Him; and He shivered on a throne on men's shoulders; and, though he was wrapped in ermine and vermilion velvet, His sad little face was pinched with frost, and His thin hand shook as He scattered apostolic benedictions. Ser Mariano gave a great shout and ran into the street with Mona Nera's foot-stool full of burning charcoal, crying that it was to warm the holy feet. The pageant stopped and cheered while He tucked it under the velvet;

and the Pontiff turned and saw us all kneeling on the doorstep—I'm sure He looked specially at me, perhaps because I was the only person present with his head swathed in a towel—and gave us a blessing apiece, each in turn, beginning with Ser Mariano. I always remember Pope Pio for that, though of course one remembers Him for all sorts of other things as well—the novel which He wrote, His noble renunciation of the Empress Leonora's love for Him when He was a young man so that she might marry the Emperor, and above all His crusade against the infidel which finally killed Him. I and Sandro ran after the pageant, as far as Santa Maria Novella; and during the next two days, until the Pontiff resumed His journey, we were always in His neighbourhood. You see we had discovered in each other the same devouring instinct for seeing things and studying the particular shapes and possibilities of them: not that we had at that time any definite idea or purpose in these proceedings—we only found that out afterwards but, at the moment, we followed our inquisitive instinct, and were excessively happy with the knowledge that we had it in common. It bound us more intimately together, if that were possible.

In this way I became one of the Filipepi household and an unindentured apprentice with Sandro in the Botticello shop. Ser Mariano had many highly respectable friends of the Ghibelline party; and we all of us wore white hose with doublets of fine white cloth over our leathern jerkins on Sundays and festivals; and were ready at all times to take a turn against those blacks the Guelfs. They were a vulgar lot, democrats, who licked the boots of the clergy and thought that no one could be a good Christian if he followed the Emperor as protector of Fiorentine liberty. Isn't the Emperor a better protector of liberty than the Pontiff Whose kingdom is not of this world. Very well then. *Suum cuique*. Every crab has his moon. And render to Caesar the things which are Caesar's and to God the things which are God's. So we Ghibellines in white followed the Emperor and venerated the Pontiff and warred with merry ferocity against the black and one-eyed Guelfs. Ser Mariano's greatest friend and patron undoubtedly was Cosimo Medici; and a most valuable connection that was. I began to know all these things after I had been about a year in the Filipepi household. First of all, of course, the Medici were enormously and inexhaustibly rich. They thought nothing of lending a hundred and twenty thousand crowns to King Edward the Fourth wherewith to recover his Kingdom of England. Churches and convents they built as a mere pastime. Why, that very year, when Cosimo's eldest surviving son Messer Piero (whom we called the Gouty) was the first Gonfalonier, they finished the church of San Lorenzo, a most chaste example of the classic manner with a doubly colonnaded cloister which you entered from the piazza. But, beside his banking business, and his trade all over the world, old Cosimo did many things, heaping up wealth incalculable with one hand, and spending it generously with the other. The books he bought, the manuscripts he collected, the learned men he purveyed from the Orient where infidel Turks were making them uncomfortable—do you know that Cosimo Medici's mercantile agents in Greece, in Asia, in Egypt, even in London, had instructions from him to collect commodities of this kind, while the captains of his galleys were forbidden to come home unless they imported at least one antique manuscript, or a sage able to teach us Fiorentines the wisdom of antique Greeks or Romans. I say nothing of intagliate gems, or of antique statues, which are too innumerable to mention. Ser Piero di Giuliano di Lapo Vespucci was one of Cosimo's captains. He had a son named Marco, the apple of his eye and just a year old at this time. Ser Piero's mother was Mona Bice Saluiati; and his father, Messer Giuliano, a rich banker and gonfalonier of justice in March and April just after Messer Piero Gottoso, was a great friend of my Sandro's father. Indeed the Vespucci and the Filipepi families were quite on friendly terms; and, though Ser Piero sailed his galley away this very year to the Levant for a three years' voyage, he was not the only Vespucci known to us. Sandro's young brother Antonio was much admired by Amerigo Vespucci. They were a queer pair—Antonio, fifteen-sixteen,—Amerigo, eight-nine—the former strictly commercial, the latter a little dare-devil. I'll tell you about the corpse which they found and sold to us presently. Messer Guidantonio Vespucci had begotten no sons of his own as yet: one came later. Wherefore he was very fond of his brother Ser Anastasio's sons, Antonio, Amerigo, and Bernardo, especially Amerigo. I don't think that Ser Anastasio was as good a man as Messer Guidantonio: he had a decent fortune of two hundred and thirty-four crowns and a decent situation as notary to the Gild of the Furriers with a salary of twelve crowns, and he lived in a decent house belonging to his brother in Borgognissanti: but the Vespucci used to say that their Ser Stagio would never set the Arno on fire; and he never did. That was left for little Amerigo. Have I said that he had an inseparable of his own age called Donato Niccolini? The tricks which those two small demons played under the instigation and with the guidance of our Antonio are almost beyond belief. What do you think of this, for example? Late in the spring, our Antonio said casually to Sandro that if he cared to stroll down to the weir outside Por al Prato he might see something worth his while. We went, of course, Sandro and I, our curiosity being excited: for Tonio already was known as a finder of strange odds and ends, generally parchments which he sold at a profit after he had let us admire them. When we came to the weir, we found Amerigo and Donato there before us, dancing like flagellants, and with them was that beautiful little Lionardo about whom Pope Pio made such a fuss when He first passed through our city. The three had their hose off and were half in and half out of the water; the river being low, as it usually is before the summer rains. On sighting us, they screeched to Toni, that something was quite safe; and he screeched back to them not to touch it for their lives. Meanwhile he ran on ahead, and peeled his legs at the river brink. Sandro and I became moved and ran too; for Toni waist-deep in the shallow stream was untying a cord which went round one of the piles of the weir; and anon he gave the end to his minions who dragged it, and a sack at the end of it, blithefully ashore. He himself came out and explained to us that, having found the corpse of some malefactor washed down to the weir in the previous autumn, he had sunk it with stones in a sack attached to the pile that the fishes might clean its bones during the winter; and this he had done because Sandro had said that he would pay a crown for a dead man's bones. Sandro got hot. If all the bones were there and clean, he said, he would buy them for a crown. If not, Toni might eat them. Toni averred that all the bones were certainly there, the malefactor not having been decapitated or mutilated but merely hanged and dragged about the streets a bit, perhaps, as was shown by the length of his neck and the shredded state of his flesh; and, as for cleanliness a whole winter under water in a swift stream—but here he got the sack open and was for pouring out its contents. Sandro roared and fell upon him; and dragged the sack with his own hands up the bank on to a level piece of turf, not wishing to lose a single one of the little pieces. As far as we could see the bones were all there, and nice and white, not black like the tarred fragments which dangle on Pol Pod. I asked Sandro how he knew the number of bones a man had. He laughed, and said that he had a habit of pinching himself in bed during sleepless nights, counting his own bones: but he added that in some parts he imagined there to be uncountable clusters of little bones, closely fitted together—the wrists, for example. But the bones, as they lay on the grass, worried me dreadfully, being all mixed up higgledy-piggledy; and I asked how they could be put together into their proper shape. Sandro snorted: there were tools in the workshop for drilling little holes: wire also could be begged or stolen; and, as for me, wasn't I a living skeleton ready to serve as a model. This made me most happy: for I would have done anything for Sandro; and I became contented with my lankiness from that instant. One thing more, though, I wanted to know, namely, what precisely was the use and purpose of the thing. And, at this, Sandro simply looked sideways at me, largely, with his big quiet masterful eyes, saying that that should be a secret between us. Toni's legs being dry, he put on his hose and inquired when he could have the crown which, he said, was to be divided between him and his assistants. Sandro answered that his money was in his box at home, not in his pouch; and payment would be made in the evening. So Toni and Amerigo and Donato were about to run away to play; but when the other little chap saw us making a bundle of the bones, he wept, saying that he also wanted a skeleton. Toni told him that he must earn a crown and buy the next one. At which Sandro was struck with an idea; and he said to his brother that he would pay half a crown for the next corpse found in the river, on condition that it was whole and fairly fresh, being desirous of cutting it to pieces with his own hands, studying the strings used by Messer Domeniddio for tying a man's bones in their places—corpse of a man or corpse of woman, it was all the same to him, though he preferred the corpse of a woman, the present one being a man. I asked him how he knew that, as we went home; and he said that the large bone in the middle of the man's body was long and narrow, but a woman's was short and broad. Sandro was the wisest person which I ever saw: but that was because he was so inquisitive. His big eyes always saw everything, all round everything, inside and outside of everything. People accused me of staring; but I never stared as awfully as Sandro. Even the mild Giovanni used to complain of it sometimes. You know they had found out almost directly that I was useful with my fingers: so a decent but awkward gawk of fifteen, one Biagio Tucci, was got to sweep the shop and to do odd jobs such as handing us the tools we cried for, while I helped Sandro and his brother with the gold work. It was interesting work, twisting and bending and chiselling bits of metal into pretty forms and joining them together in the lamp-flame: but I confess to you that both Sandro and I found the little bottles on the whole extremely irksome. What I delighted in most was getting a bit of wax and shaping it into flowers or stars: and I'm bound to say that Giovanni clouted my head more than once for cutting faces on little slabs of unground plaster. It was always Sandro's face, which I thought the most wonderful face in earth or heaven—or Lionardo's face which certainly was the face of a cherub. But, as I was saying, Sandro used to stare across the bench at me, while we were supposed to be working, till presently he made me wriggle: and then he would say that I had thirty-four teeth in my mouth or ninety-eight hairs in my right upper eyelash and sixty-five in the lower with ninety-one and sixty-four in the left, which were black where they sprang out of the flesh, brown where they began to curl and paler brown at the tips. From which I knew that his staring was not like mine and merely inquisitive, but that he was collecting and storing up knowledge as well. This came out more strongly in the putting-together of the skeleton. By the bye, we stored that under the bed in our chamber, where Mona Nera found it one day and made no end of a fuss. Indeed the whole household was upset about it. Even Giovanni said that he wouldn't have the place littered. Mona Nera's idea was that the bones ought to be properly buried. But Ser Mariano said that he didn't quite see how that could be, since the person whose they were had most likely died

under censure or in mortal sin. Mona Nera
then affirmed that they were nasty dirty things
to have in a house: at which Sandro, with his
regal red head stooped sideways and his big
eyes looking round on her, quietly conceded
that things which had been nibbled clean by
fishes and washed for a whole winter in a torrent were certainly the most nasty and dirty
and filthy and stinking things imaginable. All
which Mona Nera could say in reply was that,
if Messer Domeniddio should suddenly in-
struct His archangel to blow the last trumpet
summoning us to the Doom, it would be very
unpleasant for Sandro to have a complete
stranger, a malefactor moreover, coming into
the chamber to look for his bones. Sandro
called her a dear; and mentioned that, when
the last trumpet should sound, he would be
exclusively occupied with his private affairs
and completely indifferent to invasions of his
chamber by strangers, homicides, violent persons, evil-doers, insulters, strikers, percussors,
wounders, assassins, bandits, malefactors or
otherwise. Ser Mariano guffawed hugely, and
said that the boy was to have his way. So during
the summer we spent our spare time putting
the skeleton together with wires. For this pur-

pose, I used to let Sandro have the use of as much of my bones as he could feel with his fingers; but we both learned more of the method of framing a man from the pieces of malefactors and others to which Toni invited our attention from time to time, having fished them from the river, or (by means of his satellites) redeemed from being dragged about the streets by vulgar urchins. It was said that Luca Pitti's savage influence was still at work, seeing that so many executions took place every week, though of course the real power was passing almost entirely into the hands of Cosimo Medici. And we finished the job to Sandro's satisfaction while Messer Alessandro Machiavelli was Gonfalonier, that is to say in November, and on the day before that on which Queen Catarina of Cyprus, a fat common looking woman with a parting and fiat curtains of hair, passed through the city on her way to Rome where she was to beg for the Pontiff's help against her natural brother. I remember it because she came by Por Santamaria in going up the avenue of cypresses to visit the tomb of that young Cardinal of Lisbon who died rather than couple, as they said, and was buried at Samminiato, he being a brother of her first

*33*

husband. It was a magnificent work when it was done, our skeleton; and we put a hooked screw into the top of its head by which we hung it from a beam in our chamber, covered with an old cloak from the sight of Mona Nera when we were away in the shop. Sandro had taught me that staring at things was no good unless one made drawings of them, at the time, or immediately after, for remembrance. And we both spent our pocket-money freely with Toni, buying the scraps of paper of which he seemed to have an endless supply. It was easy enough to get a couple of silver-points, out of the filings of silver in the shop and a shaving of lead which we cut one night from the roof-lining over the attic. These, melted together in a crucible and rolled out when warm, lasted no end of a time; and, with them, we habitually noted down the shapes of things which pleased us. But, as Sandro always said, the shapes of men and women, are baffling because they change with every movement, and cannot possibly be set down by a person who does not understand the movement, which, in turn, cannot be understood by anyone ignorant of the causes of it. That is why he insisted on the skeleton as being the framework and first essential of human movement. Lifeless things were easy enough to delineate. There were two new doors of the Baptistery barely ten years old, one on the north side and the other facing Santamaria Reparata, containing numerous most beautiful figures cast in bronze and exquisitely chiselled. There was a pulpit in Santacroce covered with figures carved in marble, specially a panel of Beato Francesco and the three-crowned Pontiff Innocent, than which no work could be more admirable. These, and innumerable other things we delineated, hundreds of times, but Sandro was more diligent than I: for, strange to say, my unconquerable habit of staring had a strange effect on me. It caused me to see other things beside those at which I might happen to be staring. I understand quite well now what process was afoot then: but I am trying to explain to you how it seemed to me when I was eleven-twelve years old. It really was as though long unblinking staring, at some bronze or marble thing which we had agreed to delineate, with the two eyes in my face, opened a third eye, in some very secret part of me, wherewith my mind actually saw and observed and revelled in matters of far more ravishing and alluring phantasy than anything to be seen in the city. Then, a slap on the back from Sandro and his voice in my ear accusing me of dreaming, would shut this third eye of mine, and let me know that he had diligently covered half a dozen sheets of paper with delicate outlines, while I had not even covered two. Nothing, as I have said, could be more astonishing than Sandro's ardour in his favourite occupation. His great eyes blazed, brows straightened, lips became a line, burning red hair fell in great swathes shading his face as the lovely clear lines ran upon the paper under his nimble fingers. But he also had his periods of meditation. When we were kneeling side by side, at dawn, sometimes at Sanstefano, sometimes at Santi Apostoli, he used to let himself go free to thoughts and fancies. He knew, as well as I did, that stillness of body in beautiful or sacred surroundings conduces to visions: but he said continually, and beat me lovingly till I accepted the saying, that one might delight in such things and even strive after them but not till one's hand was trained to set down accurately and at bidding such things as one wished to set down, whether they were things which everyone might see or whether they were those things which we ourselves only could see in our imaginations. And so we strove for facility of hand, and far more diligently than to please Giovanni. You understand that Sandro and I had made up our minds that goldsmith's work was not good enough for us, and that we were to begin to paint pictures as soon as possible. Giovanni, that mild man, had no sympathy with us whatever. He made the mistake of thinking that we ought to be content. Fancy me, fancy Sandro, being content with what contented Giovanni Botticello ! Were we to be makers of little bottles all our lives? O Mary Virgin, no. Beside, the great house in Por Santamaria was getting smaller and smaller, or, rather, Sandro and I were getting bigger and bigger. Not only that. The household was increasing. Mona Nera had been producing female babies, one in my second year and another in my third. The first one she called Giulia after the celebrated Emperor of the Romans; but the second she called Benineasa after her own mother, and a very good name it turned out to be, as I shall show, for I have many things to say about these lovely girls, whose beauty is now immortal. But, what with one thing and what with another, Sandro and I were preening our feathers so to speak for flight.

Giovanni had not very much cause for complaint of our work: but we were both too large for our bed, and more or less miserable, and (in short) very liable to become a nuisance. So, on a day when all the shops were shut because our archbishop Don Orlando Bonargli died and was buried in Santamaria Reparata, Sandro went down on his knees to his father, I also being with him; and together we unfolded the causes of discomfort. Ser Mariano made to tear his hair—red like Sandro's—as he always did at the beginning, when anyone asked favours, and then, when he had made his petitioners extremely unhappy, he kissed us both and bade us speak our minds. Which we did, illustrating the same with sheaves of our delineations of beautiful things to be seen by anyone with eyes in our beautiful city and with other sheaves of delineations of living people, chiefly naked, the somewhat attenuate Toni taking a toss in the tanyard, the inseparable Amerigo and Donato knit and entwined together in schemes, or in love, or in strife, the lovely little Lionardo as Eros incorrigibly artful even in infancy and specially a delineation of Mona Nera suckling her baby Benineasa, which he declared to be verily worthy of Blessed Giovangelico of

Fiesole who brought angels to the convent of Sammarco as a bodyguard for the Mother and the Child. Also we showed him sheaves of delineations of features which hugely displeased him, delineations of assorted noses which he declared to be all awry, delineations of various mouths which he said were twisted and uneven, delineations of hands in action which he mocked at as splay-fingered, dirty nailed and as being odd ones and unpaired. Sandro and I were flabbergasted, that a man venerable for wit and scitulosity should not know that the habit of washing one 's face with the right hand in time moves all men's noses leftward at top and rightward at tip, that the uses to which we put our mouths in cursing or in praying or in ordinary cackle or in eating and drinking and holding things gives them a bias to one side or the other, and that the hand which works the most is always larger than the hand which works the least. We showed him with words—we seized blank paper and silver points and showed him with fresh delineations, that strictly correct noses and straight prim mouths and evenly matched hands are merely lifeless simulacra, and that it is precisely the cunning collocation of divergences from the rigid and symmetrical which produces that true equilibrium signifying motion and life. Indeed we spoke wonderfully, at least Sandro spoke wonderfully, I of course being his faithful echo and edging a word in here or there, saying things which we both of us knew quite well, though never before had we named them or even shaped them in words to ourselves or to each other: but it seemed that the moment was come which I suppose comes to all poets, when definitions must be made and selections of one sort or another effected. And Ser Mariano did us the justice of listening as mindfully as though we were men of his own age. Sandro declaimed: his big blazing thoughtful eyes fixed upon his father's, his white throat tensely stretched and throbbing, one arm on his father's knee and the other nimbly waving delicate explanatory fingered gesticulations, his young body writhing in eagerness, and even his muscular legs twitching like a fly's with the urgency of persuasion, till, at last, that octagonal face of his set hard, that ardent vibrant voice of his broke in a sob, beads of sweat burst out on his pure brow and his hands with a movement of pleading became still. Ser Mariano took him round the waist and drew him near, or he would have fallen so profoundly was he moved: nor was I omitted from this embrace. Sandro's father had two arms and two knees, one each for me, and one each for the son of his loins. Never let that be forgotten. And so for a space we all three nestled snugly like bugs in a rug. As for me, I clutched the good man for my life, as many a time I have clutched Sandro, when by chance we have been drowning together, with a sure and certain hope of salvation. When we were all quite happy and comfortable, Ser Mariano pronounced a judgement, just, brief, eminently satisfactory. He laughed at us for a pair of poets who could not be permitted to work half-heartedly in the shop of so exquisite a goldsmith like Giovanni any longer than was absolutely necessary. Good work was only done by willing workers; and Giovanni could find plenty of these. As for us, our exposition had been sound, and our delineations showed a couple of capable young colts who required to be caught and conditioned and bridled by some crafty condottiere. Which craftsman Ser Mariano engaged to find. Meanwhile, we were to be good boys and say our prayers and do our work in the shop as well as our consciences would let us. And that was all. I heard him telling Giovanni that same night that the eaglets were fledged. At the time I didn't understand. Now, I do. And so we went to Prato, I, and Sandro.

It seems that Ser Mariano gave himself the trouble of drinking several little beakers of wine in the workshops of various painters in the city, evenings, after he had come from the tanyard and washed and satisfied his hunger, picking their brains on our behalf. Of these Ser Andrea Verrocchio naturally was the chief. He, however, was not violently excited about us when he learned that our geniuses had not goaded us to poeticize with wax or clay, my proclivity for dough-moulding and plaster-scraping having died in the presence of paper and silver-point. He however praised our delineations: but the chief word of his which moved Ser Mariano, said on inspecting our delineations of the Bigallo, and the saint carved on Por Sangiorgio, and the house of the Wool Gild in Via Colimala and the frescoes of Palazzo delle Antolle was 'What shall these imps know of Fiorenza who know naught but Fiorenza'. Discussing this saying, and us, with his friends the Robbia, uncle and nephew, not only was Ser Mariano brought to see its wisdom, but he took also certain knowledge as to how to proceed in our business, with the result that he found a fortnight's holiday indispensable for his health; and disappeared from the city, as he usually did about that time of year, when trade was very slack, he being by no means old, extremely sturdy and fond of ordinary diversions. And on his return—they were just finishing the lanthorn of Santamaria Reparata—he presented to me and to Sandro our indentures of apprenticeship to Don Lippo our citizen and a Carmelite, who was chaplain of the convent of Santa Margherita at Prato, in which city he lived having a contract to paint the acts of Saint Stephen and Saint John Baptist on the quire of its cathedral.

I think that the first change in the nature of my friend began here. Up to this time, he was nervous and shy, because of his red hair and the notice which its beauty brought to him, though he never believed it beautiful—haughty also and impatient he was, from knowledge of his tremendous forces and the seeming lack of scope for them—wild and eccentric as people said who whirled slowly round other centres, because he was too young yet to have found out that he himself was actually a centre round which others, his adorers, of whom I (let it be noted) was the first and chief, would be only too happy to whirl—always hot and impetuous, always intimately commoved in the very marrow, in every atom of his body, in every action of his mind, in every sensibility of his soul, because, in him, at seventeen—how can I explain—well—let me tell you what the pedantic Messer Agnolo said of my friend some years later, (pedant though he was, he had insight, clear-seeing, which taught him a thing or two)— he said, quoting Plato's *Definitions*, as his habit was, that Sandro had Dexterity χαλοχαιταθια which is the habit of choosing and embracing the best things, that he had Intrepidity οφοβια which is the habit of not falling into fears, that he had Nobility εγςενεια which is the virtue of generous manners, that he had Ingenuity εγφια which is velocity in discernment and the nativity of a good nature, that he had Intelligence νοημς which is the beginning of knowledge, that he had Knowledge εηιςτηπη which is an apprehension of the mind not to be changed by reason, that he had Sensibility αςςθηυς which is an impetus of the soul and a movement of the mind, that he had Modesty ςωφρου which is simply beauty of soul, and that he would have Immortality αυαναςςα which is an ani-mated essence in a sempiternal mansion. Thus spoke Messer Agnolo of Monte Pulciano of Sandro twenty years later. It would be just to say that he had all these admirable qualities at the time when we went to Prato: he had them, as I suppose, from the moment of his baptism, but (until the time of which I speak) they were as the seeds which lie in the ground during the winter. And what I call the change of his na-ture was like the changes which seeds undergo in springtime. All the winter long they lie in the earth, hidden, bursting, shooting innumer-able ramifications of rootlets in every direc-tion unseen by mortal eye. The auspicious day comes when their angel-guardian gives them leave to concentrate their forces and break out into the sunlight. Sandro on coming to Prato was like that. Heretofore he had been using his immense forces apparently at random. Here began his springtime of concentration. When I speak of a change in his nature, I mean that. Just that.

Don Lippo was the head gardener, under whose care the seed of Sandro's genius shot up from the earth of baser things, a tender plant at first and then a strong and noble flower lifting its glory to the very empyrean. Parsons sniff a good deal about Don Lippo's morals—as though a poet's morals had anything whatever to do with his poetry: so I suppose I had better provide you with a few facts to suck before I go further. Sandro and I and most other people, his contemporaries, never saw anything of which to complain in Don Lippo's morals. I've told you that he began life as a carmelite friar. As such, he found that he could paint. The talent was encouraged in him; and he became the great spiritual painter which you know. When he was still young, and working at the convent of Santa Margherita at Prato, he fell in love with one of the nuns, Mona Lucrezia Buti. What he saw in that pinched nosed female, Heaven only knows; but no man ever does understand that sort of thing in another. I suppose Don Lippo is not the first friar who has fallen in love. He certainly isn't the last. It is so tedious to blame people who fall in love. Love is a thing which you can't help. How can you? What is one man, or one woman to do against the inherited appulse of the accumulated mentality of their millions of dead ancestors. That's what Love and Hate and all our deep sensations are, purely extraindividual. Science declares it.

Very well. Of course, as a friar and as a nun, both under vow, they were forbidden to marry. But they loved; and ran away; and certain primordial Pecksniffs seized the opportunity to moan grievously. But, by the Mercy of God, the Pontiff, Pio Secondo, was a sweet pastor. He dispensed the friar and the nun from their vows and had them regularly married, because (He said) Don Lippo was an excellent painter. O exquisite reason. Consequently there was no scandal or cause for it. The two lived very happily with their boy Pino, four years old when we came to Prato (of whom I shall speak voluminously later), and Don Lippo was chaplain of the very convent which he had deprived of Mona Lucrezia. Sandro and I lodged in his house, as did all the apprentices, and a certain Don Diamante was our rector. That one had been made a Carmelite friar at Prato by his father Ser Feo of Vuldarno, while a mere boy, and he worked with Don Lippo for love of him and for admiration of his genius. I don't call him much of a painter: which is strange, because never man had all the tricks of the trade so nearly at his fingers' ends as Don Diamante, and, yet, he never seemed able to do anything decent with his knowledge. He was a genial soul of thirty-two, free from love affairs of his own; and in fact he used to say that he was born to be other people's uncle. That about represents his situation in that life, bound by no individual ties but the friend and instructor of everybody. He certainly was a superexcellent teacher. Sandro and I of course got most of our skill from attending Don Lippo—watching luminous wonders spring to life on the plaster under his dexterous hands: but all explanations of why and wherefore, all causes which produced effects, we derived from the well-stored mind of Don Diamante. What sort of thing? This: the fashion was for females to wear their foreheads as high as a line drawn over the top of the head from ear to ear like Don Lippo's half-bald Herodias who sits at a table by herself having her chignon trimmed with grapes. Sandro and I wondered how they made their hair grow only at the back, until Don Diamante gave us the recipe for the corrosive acid with which they burned their front hair off once a month and also for the unguent with which they healed the sores on their skulls. See?

Other apprentices with us were Francesco Pinelli, a moderate and genteel man of forty, who liked to have clever or influential friends, but distinctly a gamma-double-minus painter— and Iacopo Del Sellajo, son of a Florentine saddler named Arcagnolo: he was a stolid person and a sort of old-man-of-the-sea to us for eighteen years after. And I must not omit to mention Pino di Lippo Lippi, who (at four) sat quietly with a sheaf of brushes on the scaffold behind his father, getting his fingers used to the feel of them.

Prato pleased us much. We used to say that, if we hadn't been Fiorentini, there was no other city which we would chose to live in. How different it looks today. Four hundred and forty-nine years ago it was just a fresh and simple little walled city of bell-towers, churches, palaces, and good strong houses, with a few beautiful things, each one a gem, and Donatello's boys capering on friezes everywhere. The cathedral was covered with stripes of coloured marble in the Tuscan manner, having a round and canopied pulpit with two doors on the outside angle, and wonderful bronze portals covered with bosses. Inside, there were half a dozen lovely things. Sandro immensely admired the gates of the chapel of the Sacred Girdle: hammered iron of simple circles in squares with a row of candlesticks along the top. Benedetto of Majano had done a Madonna of the Olive Tree: but we didn't think much of it. Don Lippo's new frescoes spoiled us for anything inferior. They were fine, specially a coronation of Madonna full of tall lilies standing up against the rainbow of seraphim, and a most delicious Madonna in the exsequies of San Geronimo. Later, Doffo Grillandajo did a Madonna (who looked as though made of wood) leaving her girdle to San Gianevangelista as she goes to heaven. Don Lippo had done a far better Assumption with a pope in it. But the work of his which we liked best even more than the birth of San Gianbattista and his naming was the fresco of the obsequies of San Stefano. It was done toward the end of our time in Prato, and we had by then gained enough skill to be thinking and more than thinking of doing something ourselves. Don Lippo, indeed, had let us do small things on his work at the end of our first year, such as laying the gold on the patterns which he sized. From that child's play we progressed to filling his backgrounds with appropriate colours and even to painting the dresses of his less prominent figures: but we were never allowed to try our hands at figures themselves till the time of which I speak. The master, then, being (as everyone was) amazed by the force and manner of Sandro, asked him suddenly whether his courage would serve him to paint on the Saint Stephen. Sandro nodded, and flamed, head, face, eyes. The plaster was wet. Don Lippo stepped back, and bade him cover it. With what, said Sandro. With your own mind, the master answered. Said: done. Sandro skipped up the scaffold with a new sheaf of brushes, looked over the bowls of colour which he found there and began. We all stood below, gazing at him: for the test was a terrible one. Suppose he spoiled the nearly finished fresco. But, as we gazed, from the concentrated fury of his working there came to light a portrait, a portrait do I say—a portent rather, an exact similitude of our dear Don Lippo standing at the foot of Saint Stephen's bier, and, over his shoulder, looked the ruddy round face of Don Diamante with his big black eyes and great good mouth, done, without hesitation, without consultation of the two living faces below him. That was Sandro's mind—a spontaneous act of homage to the masters who had taught him how to render them both immortal. He was twenty years old, then; and I, fifteen. I remember it because the row between the Medici and the Pitti began about that time.

We used to get our news of what was happening in Fiorenza from Ser Mariano who came to see us every year when he made his little journeys for pleasure. There was an old rivalry between those two families: but as I told you Cosimo Medici preferred the making of money and the spending it like a gentleman to worrying about the prepotence of the Pitti, specially Luca. Even when the gonfalonier knighted Luca Pitti one Christmas—it was the year when Tollo Machiavelli was born, and our Don Diamante changed from the Order of Mount Carmel to that of San Giangualberto of Vallombrosa because he wanted quiet, he said—even then Cosimo didn't even cough. The fact was that his eldest son Giovanni was lately dead and he was overwhelmed with grief. I don't think he ever cared much for Piero the Gouty, his second. I was but thirteen then, and can only tell you what I heard. But he cared a great deal for Piero Gottoso's sons, Lorenzo and Giuliano. He died, though, the year after; and wasn't able to do very much for them. What a wonderful man old Cosimo was! I'll tell you something he said as he lay a dying. He had closed his eyes for a few moments; and his wife fussily asked him why he did that. 'To see more clearly' was his answer. Don't you call that splendid. He died in the hot weather, at the beginning of August, if I remember rightly. Pope Pio was very keen on Cosimo and wrote a fine memoir of him; and then died Himself a fortnight later. Fancy a worn out old man taking the cross as a crusader and actually going on a crusade: that's what Pope Pio did; and died of it.

But, about the Medici-Pitti row—it began like this. Cosimo died; and the arrangements of his funeral, with immense pomp in San Lorenzo, were assigned to the Magnificencies of Agnolo Acciajuoli, and Diotisalvi Neroni, and Luca Pitti. A month later, the new Pope Pagolo was elected, a Vinitian called Piero Barbo, very vain; and the six priors who carried the obedience of Fiorenza to Him were the Magnificencies of Tommaso Soderini, and Luigi Guicci, and Otto Niccolini, and Filippo Medici the archbishop of Pisa, and Carolo Pandolfini and—Buonaciorso Pitti. You see how the Pitti were poking their noses into everything. Piero Gottoso, now chief of the Medici was by no means content: for, as any one could see, the citizens were sick of Pitti and asked nothing better than a strong Medici to lead them. Piero Gottoso knew this; and would have been pleased enough to take the situation: but he lacked the energy. Messer Diotisalvi Neroni had served his father well; and he left affairs to him. But Messer Diotisalvi despised the son of Cosimo; and secretly allied himself with Luca Pitti who wanted Piero Gottoso's place, with Agnolo Acciajuoli who hated all Medici, and with Niccolo Soderini who said the usual demagogic catchword 'Liberty' in reference to Fiorenza; and this crew plotted to deprive Piero Gottoso of both reputation and estate. But they had not counted on his boys, Lorenzo and Giuliano. These were frightfully inflamed at the danger threatening their family. Luca Pitti's free and daring talk, specially about getting armed help from the marquess of Ferrara, excited them enormously. They soon discovered Messer Diotisalvi's treachery and it is entirely due to Lorenzo that the conspirators failed to assassinate Piero. That was a bad year in Fiorenza, as well as elsewhere. River Arno burst its banks and inundated the city. A great star-like comet appeared under and covering the sun alarming many. Doge Francesco Sforza of Milan died and Doge Galeazzomaria succeeded him not without considerable difficulty. Lorenzo and Giuliano, therefore, set to work to buck up their father; and so excited him that the gouty galliard, using diplomatic methods arranged the elections to the Signiory in such a way that Messer Ruberto Lioni, his firm friend, emerged as gonfalonier who instantly called the citizens into the piazza to fight for the Balls of Medici. There was no fighting. Their Magnificencies of the Signiory gladly issued such bans as were required. Agnolo Acciajuoli and his two sons were banished to Barletta, Diotisalvi and his two brothers and Niccolo Soderini with his son Geri were banished to Provence, all for twenty years, while Gualtiero Panciatichi was warned to keep out of the dominion for a decade. He fled with the Neroni and the Soderini to Vinitia where most bandits go. The Acciajuoli preferred Naples. Luca Pitti remained whimpering for Piero Gottoso's clemency. What was to be done with him? Lorenzo's opinion is worth remembering. When his father consulted him, he said, He alone knows how to conquer who knows how to pardon. So the Pitti Conspiracy ended with Luca no longer prepotent but impotent, though I think that the Acciajuoli came off worst; they were perhaps the most noble of all the ferocious exquisite Fiorentini: they indeed had been doges of Athens till the Great Turk Maumetto strangled their last Doge Francesco but eight years before the Medici banned them. Donatello died that year, aged 80, and was buried in San Lorenzo near the tomb of Cosimo.

I don't think I've mentioned Donatello yet. He's the poet who did gesso work and coloured it like life. You know his lovely Saint John Baptist in Ordain-michele. He finished the bronze doors for San Lorenzo and the David which he did for Cosimo—it was the first bronze nude done since the Romans—before he died. And Lorenzo consoled his last hours by taking his favourite apprentice Bertoldo to be warden of the Medici gardens. That is only one instance of the greatness of Lorenzo. He, after the Pitti Conspiracy, went travelling with his tutor Bishop Gentile di Urbino of Arezzo, a most faithful man, as I shall have occasion to show later in dealing with another conspiracy also connected with Lorenzo. They visited Pisa, Rome, Bologna, Ferrara, Vinitia, Milan, making the young man known to princes likely to be useful or annoying to him and letting him know people with whom he would have to do when he, in his turn, became the chief of the Medici. He was much admired. Tall he was, and robust and immensely dignified. His short sight and raucous voice and total absence of the sense of smell were found attractive. He was also feared. But he was not loved. That did not matter: for as Cesare della Rovere said, it is better to be feared than to be loved—if one must choose. Lorenzo got love from us who knew him, later, as I shall tell you in due time. Just now I'm only giving you an idea of the news which Ser Mariano used to bring us when we were studying in Prato. Mona Nera kept on having babies. Giulia and Benineasa I have mentioned. Iacopo came next; and then Lorenzo, the same year when artichokes were reintroduced into Italy from Arabia and the Fiesolar Badia was finally rebuilt which was our last year in Prato.

When Don Lippo had finished his frescoes, he did a few easel-pictures just to keep his hand in until he got another job; and here it was that we got our chance. My own part, so far, now that I was expert in the grinding and blending of colours and the selection of eggs, (town eggs which have dark yolks for the darker tints, country eggs which have pale yolks for the lighter tints,) to be used as mediums, was not yet sufficiently advanced for me to attempt compositions. I could be trusted to put in washes but not to work in details; and indeed, I was still collecting details to train my hand. For a vision of my details in composition had not been granted to me. Prato was full of details, the statue with the armorials of the city on the Palazzo Pubblico of Priors, and two statues with the new arms of Medici on Palazzo Pretorio. I say new arms, because that year, King Louis of France granted to the Medici, by patent, the right to bear azure three lilies on their chief ball, so greatly did he esteem them, and the priors of Fiorenza confirmed that grant by eight beans, so greatly did Fiorenza also esteem them. Don Lippo's *Nativity* with Saint Michael and Saint Dominic seemed to me a thing to pray to: his *Slaughter of the Innocents*, his *Epiphany*, his two Circumcisions by a pope, influenced me most strangely. The churches of Prato, Santo Spirito, San Niccolo di Tolentino, Santa Maria di Buon Consiglio, San Vincenzo, San Francesco with its striped facade, San Domenico with external arches all along one side,—I believe that I could draw them even now. Then the palaces, Palazzo Pazzi, the gryphon on Palazzo Novellucci; and the city gates, Santa Trinita, Pistojese, the Via Giudea with the gate of Mercatale and its enormous Piazza. Do you know that here I got my idea of wide horizons of vast distances, which was so difficult to blend with the minute details of my compositions. I only succeeded to my satisfaction once, in all that life, in my Toby picture which I will describe in its place. But, while I was messing about in this manner, Sandro's genius was budding. Don Lippo did a Madonna, and bade Sandro and Iacopo del Sellajo to do each a Madonna of his own, having before them, for an example, his, copying it if they felt too weak to invent, or diverging from it if they wished to merit praise. Iacopo, with the presumption of twenty-three, produced a full-faced Madonna with the expression of one under the influence of a baneful electuary, and a coarse and crooked Infant with a top-knot and dirty hands. There was nothing in this work resembling the master's, excepting Madonna's magpie-sleeve. We called it a magpie-sleeve because the upper part was dark opening below to let a light undersleeve be seen; and we admired it greatly, Sandro and I, using it in most of our pictures. But Sandro's proud modesty did better than Iacopo. Modesty made him imitate Don Lippo's work: pride made him improve on it, to the master's deep delight. Madonna and Infant their pose, their aspect, their habits, he was content to take—perhaps also to refine: but whereas in Don Lippo's, Madonna's face was mixed with the rocks and trees of the high background, Sandro brought his sky down to Madonna's neck leaving her heavenly visage clear. He was a strong boy: but not precipitate.

Ser Mariano came to tell us of the birth of Giovanni Botticello's Iacopo; and It appeared that he had been blowing Sandro's trumpet in Fiorenza: for he brought a commission for a Madonna for the Foundling Hospital. Sandro said that it should be done: but, not yet presuming to trust his powers, he determined to copy and improve another work of the master's. What an improvement that was. Don Lippo's work was done with unerring touch and the skill which long experience alone can give: but his Madonna's veil was fussy and thick, her gaze vague and indecisive, her face confused with the trees and rivers and rocks of a country background: his Infant was fat, was stolid; and the angelots who held The Lord to Madonna's worship were mischievous grinning little devils of street-boys having a game with Majesty Celestial. It was a masterly work: but it was pigment. Hear how Sandro transformed it. He introduced the beautiful magpie-sleeve. He gave Madonna a sure straight gaze, an indicible purity, habits of simple and delicate transparency, brought her face against a clear sky seen through an archway, showed the Infant (a king) fumbling to undo the clasp of her mantle that He might take of her breast (O divine humanity,) made the angelot in waiting a noble who turns to see whether you, onlooker, admire your Maker sufficiently. Do you understand? Don Lippo and all other poets paint what they see with the two eyes in their face. Sandro did the same: but here he began to show us that he transcended us all, for he painted also with the eye of his mind and imagination.

Don Lippo was frightfully bucked about it and wished he had done it himself. Such a pupil, he said, must not let loyalty and modesty keep him in leading-strings any longer. Take no more from me, he said to Sandro, but compose a picture by yourself. Sandro blushed for several days at this praise; and gave himself to the grandiose plans of the very young. Oh the elaboration of the work which he initiated, a round picture, containing everything which he knew and everything else which he could think of. On a green sward with a lily pot, a timid angel supported the tottering Child to Madonna who laid her book-of-hours on the seat of a marble parapet and kneeled to worship. How ineffably pure and young she was. Over all was a monstrous tent; and two other angels opened its curtains. And beyond the terrace-parapet was a distance of trees and hills and churches and castles and sea. Sandro slaved at this work day after day for months together; and confused proportions finely. Excepting the face of Madonna, all was wrong—the tent too huge, the head of the Child too large and the legs too small, the angels purely puppets hobbled in the fussiest of involuted albes. Yes, it was a young work—sweet of course but excessively young, and Sandro said to me privately, when people spoke kindly to him, that pictures of one or two figures at most should occupy him for the present. And he said that we might try something together. I remember it, because that evening there was a sunset of mauve and gold which I think are the colours of heaven itself. And the next day Ser Mariano came with a budget of news.

Fiorenza was fairly quiet; and he wanted us to come home. There was no danger now of those nobles who had been banned the year before. The Vinitians to whom they fled, might conceivably have been a nuisance, by allying with Neroni and Acciajuoli and Soderini and Panciatichi, against us. But Carolo Pandolfini who was the first gonfalonier that year, had made friends with Medici; and he had the brilliant notion of taxing the property left by the bandits in Fiorenza to the tune of a hundred thousand florins. That stroke, of course, paralyzed them: for who ever heard of the Vinitians making alliance with anyone unable to pay ready money. Ser Mariano told of certain new works which put us in a fever to get back to Fiorenza that we might inspect them. The Robbia had been doing medallions of most beautiful swathed-babies in coloured gesso for the spandrils of the Foundling Hospital. This excited us both: for we agreed that beautiful babies were rare and none (that we had seen so far) worth being done as The Child of Madonna. It was clear, we said, that we must search for and study babies. But Ser Mariano went on. In his opinion, we were wasting opportunities in Prato. Sandro's picture had vastly pleased the Foundling Hospital and friends in Fiorenza would employ him if he were there. For example: Ser Nastagio Vespucci, actually a friend of the family, wanted his chapel painted in Ognissanti. Had Sandro been at hand, no doubt the job would have been given to him. As it was, Ser Nostagio employed one Domenico Bigordi a lad of eighteen, who certainly had done a very fine Mother of Mercy in the arch with her mantle held wide by angels to let the whole Vespucci family kneel in its folds. All this made us rather miserable through the winter. Of course we were indentured to Don Lippo as long as he remained in Prato. But the next year, he got a big job at Spoleto and Don Diamante took his place as chaplain of Santa Margherita. And being free, we scooted to Fiorenza.

Here ends the manuscript of this novel,<br>which the author left unfinished.